Poppy's Secret

Victorian stories linking with the History
National Curriculum.

Sch

First published in 1996 by Franklin Watts
Paperback edition published 1997
This edition 1998

Franklin Watts
96 Leonard Street
London EC2A 4RH

Franklin Watts Australia
14 Mars Road
Lane Cove
NSW 2006

Series editor: Paula Borton
Consultant: Joan Blyth
Designer: Kirstie Billingham

A CIP catalogue record for this book
is available from the British Library.

ISBN 0 7496 2634 8 (pbk)
0 7496 2374 8 (hbk)

Dewey Classification 942.01

Printed in Great Britain

Poppy's Secret

by
Mary Hooper

Illustrations by Leslie Bisseker

W
FRANKLIN WATTS
LONDON • NEW YORK • SYDNEY

1

A Feathery Task

"Not done yet?" Cook roared. She stood in the doorway of the scullery and glowered at Poppy. "What have you been doing all morning?"

Poppy, who was standing shivering at the stone sink and trying not to feel sick,

didn't reply. She'd been given eight chickens to pluck and prepare for the family lunch upstairs that day and was having trouble doing them. Every minute or so she had to stop and blow on her fingers to warm them, for it was freezing cold in the scullery.

"You're useless! Give one here!" Cook pushed Poppy out of the way and made quick stabbing motions to pull out the

chicken's feathers. "Like this – see. And when the skin's clear then you break its legs and cut its head off..."

Cook raised her heavy knife in the air and Poppy closed her eyes and shuddered. She'd always hated doing messy, gory jobs – even at home.

Home. Poppy felt sad when she thought that word, because she didn't really know where home was any more.

When her dad had lost his job on the farm, the family had moved to a place in a grimy city, Morchester, that Poppy had never seen. Poppy had a job as a scullery maid in rich Lord Throckmorten's house, so when the Lord's household moved from London to their big house near Morchester, Poppy had thought she'd be able to go and see Ma and her seven brothers and sisters. She hadn't managed it yet, though, scullery maids didn't have much money – or time – for visiting!

Her dad was working away on the railways now, and four of her brothers and sisters had left home and were apprenticed at the nearby cotton mill, also owned by Lord Throckmorten. Home, then, and everything about it, had changed.

Poppy was reminded where she was by a shove in the back from Cook. "Now get on! If they aren't finished in half an hour you'll be in trouble, Miss."

Poppy sighed and got on. An hour later, she went into Cook's parlour to tell her they were done and then stood by the kitchen range for a moment, holding out her red-raw hands to the heat to try and warm them.

"You'll catch it standing there!" Jack
the footman said. "If Mr Grange sees

you standing idle he'll give you the silver to polish."

Poppy poked out her tongue in the direction of the butler's, Mr Grange's, parlour. "I hate it here!" she said. "Everyone's horrible to me."

"You want to think yourself lucky you're not working at the Mill," Jack said. "I've heard it's awful bad there. At least we get food and a proper bed to sleep in here – that's more than they get. Why, I've heard that sometimes they have to sleep under the machinery on sacks!"

Poppy frowned indignantly. "Doesn't Lord Throckmorten know that? Why doesn't he look after his workers better?"

"He's only interested in the money," Jack said in a low voice.

"Is it really that bad?" Poppy asked, picking bits of feather off her apron. "Only, my brothers and sisters are working there. Alfred and George, Lily and Rose," she added with a sigh, for she really missed them sometimes.

Jack put down the boots he was polishing. "It's about as bad as it could be. If they've a big order for cloth on they keep the weaving looms going full time and then they have to work all night.

It's dangerous, too. People get caught in the machinery and get injured and no-one seems to care."

Poppy gasped. She'd had no idea it was so awful. "How far is it to the Mill from here?"

Jack shrugged. "It's way over the hills. It takes a good couple of hours to walk it – I had to go there once on an errand for Master." He looked at her intently. "You're never intending to go!"

"Would you be able to draw me a map of how to find it?" Poppy asked.

"Reckon I could," Jack said. "But you won't like what you see. Best not to know, I reckon."

Poppy's eyes glinted. "I'm the oldest in the family and Ma's always expected me to look out for my brothers and sisters. Now you've told me about the Mill, I think I ought to go and see it for myself."

Jack puffed out his cheeks. "Well, if you get caught, don't let on it was me who told you how to get there."

"Don't worry," Poppy said. "I won't get caught!"

Mill

Lord Throckmorten's house

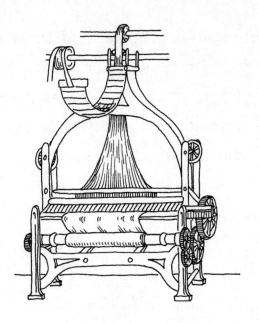

2

Danger at Work

Poppy, by standing on a wall outside the Mill, could just about see through a grimy window into the vast weaving shed.

The shed was long and high, more like a massive barn, and filled with the huge looms which spun the cotton. About thirty of them stood, whirring and clanging, vibrating and crashing. Even from outside where Poppy was, the noise was deafening.

She could barely see inside, for it was poorly lit and the air was filled with flying specks of cotton and dust.

After a few moments, though, she managed
to make out the huddled forms of children
crouched under the machines. Every so
often one of them would scurry or
crawl further under to adjust
something, disappearing right
into the loom.

Poppy made her way along, looking anxiously through the windows. Were things really as bad here as Jack the footman had said? Where were Alfred and George, Lily and Rose?

She didn't have much time to look for them. That morning she'd got up at five as usual and done all her chores, then, crossing her fingers, pretended to the housekeeper that she had bad stomach pains and needed to go back to her room and rest.

Once upstairs, she'd changed into her oldest clothes, borrowed a black cloak for warmth and set off for the Mill, following Jack's map.

The wailing sound of a siren made Poppy jump, but she stayed where she was and watched as, inside the shed, the machinery came to a grinding, shuddering halt. One by one, a stream of small, grubby children began to appear, coming out of nooks and crannies and hidey-holes among the machines, stretching and yawning, rubbing their eyes.

Poppy jumped down from the wall and slid, as silently as a shadow, round the corner of the shed and towards the doorway that the children were making for.

The children poured outside and began lining up by a trestle table, pushing and shoving each other for a place. As each reached the front, they were given a small baked potato and a chunk of greyish bread. When they were all served, Poppy moved into the middle of them, looking for the familiar faces of her brothers and sisters.

She found the twins, Lily and Rose, quite easily. They were tiredly squabbling over who had the biggest potato and squealed with pleasure on seeing her.

"Have you come to work here now?" Lily asked.

"Pity you if you have!" said Rose.

"Is it that bad?" Poppy asked.

"It's awful," Lily said, stuffing potato into her mouth and then hungrily eyeing Rose's.

Rose took little bites out of her potato, looking at Poppy as if she couldn't quite believe she was there. "Don't come and work here unless you have to," she said. "The overseer – that's the man in charge – is cruel and beats us for nothing."

Poppy put an arm around Rose's thin shoulders. "Where are Alfred and George?" she asked. Lily wriggled herself under Poppy's other arm. "Alfred's carding cotton in another shed," she said, "we don't see much of him. George is poorly."

"He was crying so much this morning

that we had to leave him in the apprentice house."

"Where's that?" Poppy asked.

"It's that big place there," Rose pointed to an ugly grey building a short distance away. "It's where we live."

"George has hurt his arm," put in Lily. "He caught it under one of the machines yesterday."

Poppy looked at them in horror. "But what will happen to him?"

They both shook their heads.

"Dunno," said Rose.

"Can't he see a doctor?"

"We never see anyone like that here!" Lily said, quite astonished. "Anyway, he'll have to come to work tomorrow, otherwise he'll get beaten."

Poppy took a deep breath. It seemed she'd arrived just in time. "Where is he now? How can I find him?"

As she spoke the siren wailed out again and Lily and Rose crammed the last of their bread into their mouths.

"We've got to go!" Lily said. "We daren't be late in!"

"Tell me where George is first!" Poppy said urgently.

"Are you going to take him away?"

Lily asked.

"Will you take us away, too?" Rose asked wistfully.

"First things first," said Poppy. "Now, exactly where can I find George?"

"In the boys' room – upstairs in the apprentice house," Lily said. "George is hiding under some straw. But you'll get into awful trouble if anyone —"

"Oh, I'll be all right!" Poppy said, thinking to herself that it was no joke being the oldest in the family...

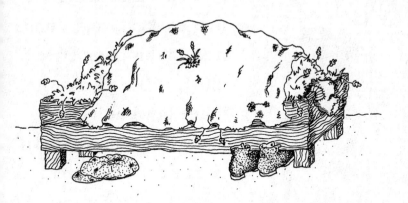

3

Escape

Poppy looked through the window of
the apprentice house and found herself
staring into a long, bleak room lined with
tables and benches.

"Eating room," she muttered to herself.
She crept along a little further and came

to another room, a
kitchen with a black
iron cooking range, and
next to this another,
much larger room, with
a line of what looked
like wooden boxes down
each side. These were so
close that they were
touching each other.
Each one contained a
heap of straw and a
raggedy sheet.

"Girls' bedroom," Poppy muttered.

In the corner of the room was a
wooden ladder. This must lead, Poppy
decided, to the boys' room upstairs.

Keeping low, she crept back towards
the kitchen, where the door into the house
was. Peering through the window again,

28

she saw a stout woman in an apron,
asleep on a chair, a cooking pot clutched
in her arms.

Poppy stood for a while wondering
what to do, and then decided – for the
cook was snoring loud enough to be heard
outside – that she was sleeping deeply
enough to risk creeping past her.

Walking on tiptoe, holding her breath,
Poppy slipped past the sleeping figure.

There was a bad moment when a shout from someone outside made the cook stir, but she managed to make her way through to the girls' room undisturbed.

She crept up the rickety ladder and came into a large, dark room twice the size of the girls' room.

"George!" she called in a harsh whisper. "George! Are you here?"

There was no reply. She called again and after a few seconds a frightened voice said, "Who is it? Who's that?"

"It's me. It's your sister Poppy!"

There was a rustling of straw from one of the middle beds as someone moved. "Here I am," the voice whimpered. "Oh, Poppy, I'm hurt!"

George burst into tears and Poppy rushed over to him.

"Don't touch me!" he said between sobs.

"It's my arm. I think it's broke!"

Poppy pulled a face as she looked at his arm, which was bruised and bloody and sticking out at a funny angle.

"Have you shown this to anyone?" she asked.

George shook his head. "There's no-one to show. We got a warden, but he only comes in once a week. It hurts bad and I

don't know what to do!" George's tears dropped onto the straw. "It's awful here, Poppy. And Ma has signed us up for eight years!"

"Ma never would have done that if she'd known what it was like here," Poppy said with certainty. "And she'd come and get you out herself now if she knew you were hurt."

George continued to sniff and sob while Poppy considered what was to be done. She knew children could be beaten – and even put in prison – if they ran away from their mill jobs. And anyone who helped them would be in trouble, too. But she couldn't just leave him here.

There were voices downstairs and Poppy crept to the edge of the room and looked down the ladder. Cook was awake and had visitors, it seemed. People were talking in the kitchen and there was the clink of cups being put out. Cook was about to have a tea party – and that meant Poppy and George couldn't get past them and out of the door without being seen!

Poppy walked all round the room and looked out of the window. "How's your

other arm? Your good arm?" she asked
after a moment.

"All right," George sniffed. "But what
are we going to do?"

"You'll see," Poppy said.

She took George's thin
sheet off his bed and very
carefully with much
whimpering from George
tied his bad arm flat
to his body, so it
wouldn't move. Then
she helped George
over to the window,
which luckily was
set low in the wall,
making the drop
to the ground quite a short one.

She took off her big cloak.

"You've got to hold on tightly to one end

of this with your good hand," she explained to George, "while I lower you out of the window."

It took a lot of persuasion before George would do this, but in the end he agreed. With George safely on the ground outside, Poppy began to lower herself out. She almost lost her nerve when it came to actually letting go of the ledge, but when she heard somone coming up the ladder it was the final prod she needed. She let go and landed safely on the ground beside George.

He was whimpering with cold, pain and fright all the way back to the Throckmorten's house. "I daren't run away," he kept crying. "If anyone finds out, I'll get beaten."

"No-one will find out. You're my special secret," Poppy said, deep in thought. She had two problems – to get George to a doctor and then to get him safely home to Ma. Whatever happened, she couldn't let him down.

4

Poppy's Secret

"You've done what?!" Jack's face was a picture.

"I had to," Poppy said. "I think he'd have just lain there for ever otherwise. No-one was looking after him! He might have died if I hadn't got him away."

It was now the evening and supper had been eaten and served at the big house. Poppy, recovered from her "stomach cramps", had just finished scrubbing down the kitchen tables. She'd snatched a quiet moment to talk to Jack while the rest of the servants went about their evening chores.

"Where's he hiding now, then?"

Poppy grinned. "In the broom cupboard in the hall," she said. "It's all right," she added as Jack started to make a fuss. "I've told him not to make a sound."

"But what are you going to do with him?

He can't stay in the broom cupboard for ever!"

"I know…" Poppy looked down for a moment. "It's a pity Miss Isabella isn't here – she's been really nice recently. She might have helped."

"The fewer people in on the secret, the better!" Jack said. "You especially don't want them upstairs to know."

"I gave George something to eat, then the poor wee thing just went in the cupboard and went to sleep," Poppy said. "I must try and get him to a doctor, though – his arm looks awful. I think I saw a bone sticking out."

Jack shook his head. "You've got yourself in a right pickle, haven't you?" He thought for a moment. "You'll have to take him to the poor ward at the hospital," he said. "That's the only place that folks like us can get to see doctors and nurses."

"How do I get there?" Poppy asked, thinking to herself that it was just one thing after another.

"It's in the city – twelve miles away," Jack said. "You won't be able to walk it."

"And even if I could, George couldn't," said Poppy.

Jack lowered his voice. "I've got a bit of money saved up," he said gruffly. "If you want, I could lend you the fare."

"Could you?"

Jack looked serious. "If you go from here, they won't have you back, you

know," he said. "Especially when they realise you've helped your brother run away from the Mill."

Poppy nodded grimly. "I've thought of that. After we've been to the hospital I reckon we'll just have to take ourselves straight home to Ma."

Jack nodded. "When will you go?"

"I'd like to be off tonight," Poppy replied, "but George could do with a rest."

"You could do with a rest yourself," Jack said. "If I were you I'd go first thing in the morning before anyone's up."

"What, just go – without cleaning the range and raking out the fires?!"

Poppy asked mischievously.

Jack grinned. "Leaving the ashes will be the least of your sins," he said. "Tell you what – I'll get the money and meet you on the back stairs at five o'clock."

The housekeeper came in just then and eyed Jack and Poppy suspiciously. "What are you two gossiping about?"

Poppy bobbed a curtsey to her. "Just a little secret of mine, Ma'am."

"Scullery maids have no business having secrets," the housekeeper sniffed. "In my day —"

There was a sudden crash and clatter from outside in the hall – from the broom cupboard where George was hiding!

"What on earth's that?" the housekeeper said, making for the door. "Things falling over because they've not been put away properly, I'll be bound. Sloppy housekeeping —"

Poppy ran to the broom cupboard and stood in front of it. "Sorry, Ma'am. I'll tidy everything. I'll do it now."

A small sigh came from inside the cupboard and Poppy quickly turned away from the housekeeper and made a meowing noise. "Sounds like one of the cats has got in there!" Poppy said. "I'll sort things out. Leave it to me!"

45

Jack coughed loudly. "I wonder if I could take this opportunity to ask you about my future prospects," he said to the housekeeper. "I thought that someone so experienced as yourself would be best placed to advise me..."

As Jack spoke, he opened the door back into the kitchen and ushered the housekeeper through it. Poppy sighed with relief. So far, so good...

5

A Long Wait

Poppy was tired, cold – and very
worried about George. He seemed to be
in a daze, coming to himself only slightly
whenever Poppy urged him to drink some
of the milk she'd bought on their way to
the hospital.

They'd got away from the house
safely, then hitched a lift on a wagon to
the nearest town. After that Poppy had
used some of Jack's money to take a
horse-drawn omnibus into the city. It was
only the second time Poppy had ridden in
one, but she was too worried about
George to enjoy the trip.

The hospital they were in
was a grim, dark building.

Poppy thought it looked a bit like a workhouse. Inside it was damp and dingy and crowded with sick and injured people waiting to be seen. The ones who'd arrived early sat on benches, the rest were sitting or lying on the floor, patiently waiting for the one doctor on duty. Many of them had hard, racking coughs, and occasionally there was a shout from someone in pain, but other than that it was just the odd groan that broke the silence.

It was nearly four hours before Poppy and George were seen. They were taken into a side room and a nurse came in and gently removed first the blanket, then George's thin shirt, and began to examine his arm.

Poppy felt shy and embarrassed. She'd never even seen a nurse before, let alone been in a hospital, but for George's sake she knew she had to be very grown-up and sensible.

"How long ago did you do this?" the nurse asked, touching the wound gently.

"Two or three days back," Poppy answered for George. "He caught it in machinery at the Mill."

The nurse shook her head. "Another day and it would have gone septic. You did well to bring him in."

"Is it broken?" Poppy asked.

The nurse nodded. "And quite a bad break, too. I'll get the doctor along to set it and we'll get you something against the infection." She patted George on the head. "You'll be fine. Your arm will be put in a sturdy wooden splint, but you must try to keep it as still as possible. And it must be kept clean."

"Will he —" Poppy began, and then gasped, her attention caught by the fine gold watch that the nurse had pinned to her white apron. A watch with a clover emblem!

Ages ago, Ma's family had been rich. One day there had been a big family row, so great-grandmother had hidden her money and told her four grown-up children that they'd only get it if they made friends. They were each given a watch or locket containing a golden key and one line of a riddle.

The nurse smiled. "I see you've noticed my lovely watch," she said. "It was given to me by a grateful patient. Isn't it beautiful?"

Poppy nodded breathlessly. "Is it... has it got some words written inside?"

"Indeed it has!" the nurse said in surprise. "But how did you know that?"

"Because our Ma had a locket like it!" Poppy said. "There were four pieces of jewellery, all with a line of a riddle inside. If you get all four lines and solve the riddle then it's supposed to lead you to treasure!"

The nurse laughed. "I don't know about that," she said. She looked thoughtful for a moment, "But now you've told me, the old chap who gave it to me did say something about a treasure. He said it was to be found in London, near St Paul's Cathedral."

"Could...do you think you could tell us what your clue says?" Poppy asked.

"I should think I could," said the nurse, "since I'm much too old to go treasure-hunting myself. But what are your lines?"

"*Where life's torch flames burn no more,*

And the urn is covered o'er" Poppy said eagerly.

The text on the watch reads: *"Where Hope waits, bowed down with Sorrow,"*

"And mine is, *Where Hope waits, bowed down with sorrow,* – whatever that means!" said the nurse. "If you find out, mind you come back and give me a share of that treasure!"

"I'll do that," Poppy promised. She nudged George, "Isn't it exciting!" she said – but George was asleep again.

"Best thing for him," the nurse said. "After his arm's been set I should try and sleep on the benches here tonight, then you can get off home in the morning."

6

Home!

It was late afternoon by the time Poppy
and George reached their Ma's house.
It was in a row of tiny brick-built houses
crammed back-to-back with scores
of others.

Ma's face was a picture of amazement

when they appeared. "Poppy and George!" she cried. "Why, whatever's happened?!"

Poppy explained how she'd gone on a secret visit to the Mill and found George injured. "He can't go back, Ma!" she said. "You'll have to hide him here."

Ma held out her arms to George. "He's never going back there!" she cried.

"We're a bit pushed here, but we'll manage somehow."

Poppy hugged her Ma. This wasn't the right time to tell Ma that she'd come home to live, too.

Her sister Marigold came in carrying Daisy, and Poppy gasped in surprise. "Haven't they grown!"

Daisy, who'd been a baby in arms when Poppy had left home, didn't recognise her and began to whimper. Even five-year-old Marigold, who was covered in coal dust, didn't know her at first and bobbed a curtsey at this smartly dressed young woman speaking to her Ma.

"You don't curtsey to me – I'm your sister!" Poppy said,

and she made a grab to catch hold of Marigold. Marigold, however, wriggled away and made for the stairs at the back of the room. She sat there with Daisy on her lap, watching Poppy, wide-eyed.

There was a wail from outside and Poppy whirled round. "I'd almost forgotten about the new baby!"

"He doesn't stay forgotten for long," Ma said, and she went outside and came back holding a rough wooden box containing a squealing, red-faced infant.

"This is Albert. Your brother," she said, putting the box on the floor and plonking the baby in Poppy's arms.

59

Poppy smiled down at him. "I'm glad he's got red hair like me," she said, stroking his head. "None of the others have."

"Then let's hope he has your luck as well," Ma said. "He'll need it."

Albert stared up at Poppy and his pudgy hand reached round her neck for the key he could see hanging there. Poppy took it off and gave it to him to play with.

"You're not still wearing that!" Ma exclaimed.

Poppy nodded. "I've got the next line of the riddle, too. I promised you, didn't I – some day I'm going to solve the riddle and find that treasure!"
She yawned widely.
"But not yet," she added. "Because right now I'm going to sleep for at least a week!"

Victorian working life

Houses for the workers

In Victorian times, masses of cheap slum housing
went up very quickly. Often these houses were built
"back to back", which meant there were no
windows in the back of the house and no garden
or yard, either. There were no bathrooms and the
only water was from a pump in the street.
Sometimes up to twelve families had to share this –
and share the lavatory, too.

Child labour

Large families were so expensive
to keep that often parents
would "apprentice" their childre

for up to twelve years. This meant that they were supposed to be trained to do a job. In fact, this didn't often happen. Instead, like Poppy's brothers and sisters, they'd be put to work for long hours and receive little more than their food and lodging. Those, like Poppy, who worked in a big house "in service" were luckier, but unless you were rich you really wouldn't have wanted to be a child in Victorian times!

In the mill

Children like Poppy's brothers and sisters often worked twelve or fourteen hours a day at the Mill – longer if there was a demand for cloth. They had the barest amount to eat, just enough to keep them going. They were supposed to get some schooling, but were usually so tired that they fell asleep over evening lessons. The 1847 Factory Act said that children should not work more than ten hours a day, but greedy factory and mill owners often didn't take any notice of this. Gradually, though, more laws were passed and slowly things improved.

Hospitals

There was no National Health Service so hospitals were usually run by charities. If you couldn't pay to have a doctor visit you at home, you had to go along and wait - and wait and wait - at a hospital casualty ward. It wasn't until Florence Nightingale began her training school in the 1850s that women nurses were seen as respectable and valuable, but even then the first female doctor (Elizabeth Garrett Anderson) didn't qualify until 1870.